Somebody Moved in Next Door

Story by Janet Slater Bottin

Illustrations by Pat Reynolds

Contents

Chapter 1

A New Neighbor

Once I lived on the most boring street in town. On one end lived the "small fry" — little kids. At the other end were the "big fish" — teenagers. Living in the middle was... me. Just me. None of my friends lived *anywhere* near.

Sure, I saw them at school. But *after* school … BOREDOM. Nothing to do — no one to hang out with. Just me in the middle. Alone. The only eleven-year-old kid on the street.

Then the neighbors moved out from next door. For weeks I watched their house and waited, and hoped…

Finally, a moving van arrived, followed by a minivan.

A man and a woman climbed out of the front of the minivan. Then somebody wearing jeans and a sweatshirt climbed out of the back.

I couldn't tell if it was a girl or boy. But I didn't care much. The main thing was that this "somebody" looked the right age. My age!

In the middle of this great event in my life history, Mom called me inside to get ready for my dentist appointment! I begged her to try to change the appointment time, but Mom just couldn't see how the arrival of new neighbors with a right-sized "somebody" could be more important than drillings and fillings.

I didn't get to see that kid again until after I got home from school the next day. The kid was wandering up and down in the front yard next door, peering at the ground. You could tell he'd lost something — or maybe *she'd* lost something.

I still couldn't figure out whether it was a girl or boy...

I'm a sociable person — mostly. I make friends easily — usually. So I decided to be my mostly sociable, usually friendly self and call out to that kid "Hi there!" I yelled. "My name's Charlie. I live next door." (Which was pretty obvious.)

The kid didn't even look up! It was as if I didn't even exist! So I tried again.

"Hey!" I bellowed. "As I said, my name is Charlie. What's yours? Have you lost something? Can I help you find it?"

How did that kid respond to my offer? It marched up the sidewalk into its house and *slammed the door!* I was flabbergasted. I was outraged. I was *furious.*

All the years I'd waited for a friend to move in next door, and when I finally thought I might have one, what did I get? *A snob.*

"I know what you've lost!" I yelled. "Your manners! And maybe your brain as well."

I told my friends all about our new snooty neighbor at school the next day.

"What a jerk," sniffed Becky.

"You can say that again," said Carlos.

"What a jerk," said Becky.

"Don't waste your time worrying about it," said Tan. "We've got more important things to think about — like the Recycling Competition..."

The Recycling Competition had been organized by a local environmental group. It was a team project for school children to make

a model out of recyclable garbage, and a poster about recycling. First prize for all age-groups was a ride in a helicopter. We *really* wanted that ride!

We had only three weeks left to finish our project — and we hadn't started. We just couldn't agree about what to use and make. Carlos wanted to use pop cans. Becky wanted to use popsicle sticks because she had lots of them. And Tan wanted to make papier-maché models.

I just wanted everyone to make up their minds, so I could get started on *my* job... the poster.

"We've just got to make a decision," sighed Becky.

"You can say that again," said Carlos.

"We've just got... "

"Can it, Becky," said Tan.

"That's just what I want to do — 'can' it!" said Carlos.

We were getting nowhere. We "canned it" and went home.

Chapter 2

Get Your Paws Off My Cat!

I could feel I was being watched as I came in our gate. That next-door kid was outside again.

It *grinned* at me. Then it *waved!*

"Great grasshoppers!" I thought. "The alien is trying to make contact now! Should I respond?"

I was still feeling mad about the way that kid had snubbed me yesterday. I decided it should be ignored in the same way it had ignored me.

I ignored it all the way up the sidewalk to my house, and then sneaked another quick look as I slid through the door. The kid was just standing there, looking stunned.

"Ha, ha!" I thought. "One for me! We're even now…"

My mom's voice suddenly shattered my smugness. "Charlie, is that you? Could you run next door for me, please?"

She explained, "I've just glanced through today's mail, and there's a stray letter among ours. I think it must be meant for our new neighbors. Take it over now, before you do anything else, okay? It might give you an opportunity to meet the new child next door."

I groaned inside myself. If only Mom knew — the *last* thing I needed was an opportunity to meet that far-out, bad-mannered weirdo.

I slunk back outside with the letter. Phew! The kid was nowhere in sight. I didn't actually need to deliver this letter *personally*, I thought. "I could shove it in their mailbox! Brilliant!"

I crept along the fence to the mailbox. The kid was under the mailbox, crouching down, stroking a cat. He (or she) didn't know I was there. The cat was *my cat*, Frisby. He was purring loudly.

I shrieked, "Hey! You! Get your paws off my cat!"

The kid IGNORED ME — but not for long! I threw down the letter and grabbed Frisby. The kid teetered and tumbled backward into the yard.

I marched off triumphantly with Frisby.

That kid would know better in the future than to ignore ME.

I told the other kids all about it the next morning while we were hanging around together before school.

"You got that snobby kid back big time," said Becky.

"You can say that again," said Carlos.

"You got..."

"Oh, NO!" I gasped. "Don't look now, but that's the kid's mother coming out of the school office and that — *that is* THE KID."

Of course they all looked. The kid was wearing a skirt.

"She's a girl," said Becky.

"She's a PAIN," I said. "What if she ends up in our class? We should warn everyone what she's like."

Chapter 3

A Boy or a Girl?

Rumors always spread around our school like wildfire. This one traveled super-fast. By the time school started, everyone would have heard that my next-door neighbor was a bad-mannered weirdo.

Our teacher, Mrs. Pinney, called the class to order. "Listen, everyone," she said, "we have a new student joining our class today. She'll be here shortly, but first there's something I need to tell you about Jodie."

"Yeah. She's a snob," I hissed to Becky.

Of course, that wasn't what Mrs. Pinney wanted to say.

"You won't be able to communicate with Jodie in the usual way," said Mrs. Pinney. "Jodie is hearing-impaired but there are three ways in which you can communicate with her. She lip-reads very well. If you want to speak to Jodie, you must be facing her so she can read your lips. Don't speak too fast."

Mrs. Pinney went on. "Another way of holding a conversation with Jodie is by writing messages. And the third way is through sign language — remember, we learned some sign language earlier this year?"

As Mrs Pinney continued, my mind was slowly matching this information to my memories of trying to communicate with Jodie. I hadn't been facing Jodie when I'd spoken to her. She hadn't seen me. She hadn't *heard* me.

I glanced at Tan and Carlos and Becky. They were looking at me. I could tell they were thinking the same thing...

Jodie hadn't behaved badly toward me at all. It was *I* who'd behaved badly toward *her*. *Really* badly. *I'd* been the BAD-MANNERED SNOB.

I'd snubbed her when she'd tried to be friendly. I'd grabbed my cat from her in a fit of jealous rage. I'd said ugly things about her, and spread untrue rumors around the school. I felt *sooooo* bad. I felt even worse a moment later, when Jodie walked into the classroom.

Mrs. Pinney introduced her to the class. Jodie glanced around, kind of smiling, kind of nervous.

I tried to make myself invisible. It didn't work. She stared at me. I could feel her looking. I felt so ashamed and guilty about the way I'd behaved, I couldn't meet her eyes.

I watched Mrs. Pinney talking to Jodie. She spoke more slowly and distinctly than usual. Mrs. Pinney asked Jodie if there was anyone in particular she'd like to sit next to. I risked a quick peek over my book. Jodie was pointing — straight at ME.

I gasped. So did Tan and Carlos and Becky. They knew all the mean things I'd done and said. I guessed they were thinking exactly what I was…

Of all the people in the room, why would Jodie choose to sit beside ME?

"I'm sure we can make some room beside Charlie," smiled Mrs. Pinney. "We'll just need to rearrange the chairs a little."

While Mrs. Pinney reorganized the chairs, I tried to reorganize my mind! My head couldn't get around the fact that Jodie had chosen to sit next to me.

Mrs. Pinney finished rearranging the room, and Jodie slid into the chair next to mine.

"Now what?" I thought. I sneaked a nervous glance at her. She looked toward me and *smiled*.

I couldn't stand it — why was she being so friendly when I'd been so snooty? I grabbed a scrap of paper and scribbled, "Why are you being so nice? I've been a real pig to you." I shoved it toward her.

She read it and wrote back, "Yes — you have. But I thought you were worth another try. There's nobody else my age on our street."

Jodie was grinning at me again, with a big question in her eyes. I grinned back, sheepishly.

She scribbled another note. "I didn't get what the teacher said your name was."

"Charlie," I spelled out in sign language. Her eyes widened in surprise.

Quickly she wrote again, "Are you a boy or a girl?"

I stared down at my jeans and T-shirt and raked my hands through my short, curly hair. Then I laughed so loudly that all the kids in the class stopped working and stared.

"I am a girl," I signed. Then I grabbed the pencil again and scribbled, "Charlie is short for Charlene. I didn't know that you were a girl, either, until I saw you wearing a skirt this morning!"

Jodie read it, then *she* laughed, too. At that point, Mrs. Pinney interrupted our conversation by plonking some work down in front of us both, and telling me I should postpone getting acquainted with Jodie until recess.

Chapter 4

Brilliance × Wow!

Tan and Carlos and Becky couldn't wait to get acquainted, too.

Jodie could read our lips really well, like Mrs. Pinney had said. If we spoke too fast, she'd ask us to repeat ourselves, and she taught us to tap her arm lightly to get her attention before we spoke. We could even do a little bit of signing. We talked a lot about each other, and I liked everything I found out about Jodie.

During the afternoon, Mrs. Pinney told the class we could all have an hour to work on our recycling projects.

Then she asked, "Who would like to include Jodie in their team?"

Carlos, Tan, Becky, and I shot our hands up simultaneously.

"All right," smiled Mrs. Pinney. "You're the 'pop can' team, aren't you?"

"We haven't decided yet," mumbled Tan. "It could be paper or popsicle sticks."

"Very well, Jodie can join the 'undecided' team," said Mrs. Pinney crisply. "And they had better decide on a topic quickly."

The first thing we did was explain our "undecidedness" to Jodie. She thought for a very long time. Then she signaled for a pen and some paper.

She wrote all the options down:

Artwork	Charlie
Popsicle sticks	Becky
Pop cans	Carlos
Newspaper	Tan

Then she added to her list:

Artwork	Charlie — design and paint poster with slogan "Don't ham things up! Keep the scene clean. RECYCLE."
Popsicle sticks	Becky — design and make a pigsty
Pop cans	Carlos — make two feeding troughs (borrow my dad's tin snips)
Newspaper	Tan — make four papier-mâché pigs

Finally, I grabbed her pen and scribbled on the bottom of the list:

Brains	Jodie — brilliance x wow!

We grabbed Jodie's hands and danced her around.

"I gather you've finally reached a team decision," said Mrs. Pinney. "So how about starting some serious work?"

Now that we knew what we were doing, we were ready to start work very seriously. We really wanted that helicopter ride!

Jodie suggested we begin by each planning our separate tasks.

Becky drew designs for a popsicle pigsty. Tan organized what he needed for four papier-maché pigs. Carlos planned how to convert pop cans into pig troughs. I drew a rough outline of my poster.

We were all excited about each other's ideas. But mostly we were excited about having Jodie on our team. We were amazed by her incredible imagination. Not only did she have the greatest ideas herself, but she got the rest of us thinking and imagining as well.

Chapter 5

If Pigs Could Fly...

Becky tapped Jodie's arm for attention. "What are you doing for the project, Jodie?" she asked curiously. "What arc you writing?"

Jodie handed us some pieces of paper.

PIG POEMS

1. This little pig went to market.

   This little pig wrote a poem.

   This little pig recycled

   And cleaned up its home.

2. "Little pig, little pig, let me come in."

   "No, not by the hair of my chinny-chin-chin,

   unless you recycle your plastic and tin."

3. If pigs could fly across the sky,

   And see the world from way up high,

   I wonder if they'd see a mess.

   I wonder if they'd rightly guess

   The mess was made by you and I?

   I wonder if they'd wonder why.

4. Higgety Piggety my fat sow

   Wasn't very tidy until I taught her how.

   Once she had a stack of bottles and tins.

   Now she puts her 'empties' in recycling bins.

"You wrote these poems? Just now?"
We gasped. This girl was extraordinary!

"You could make them into picket signs with popsicle sticks," suggested Becky. "And plant them around our pigsty!"

"I'd like to use the flying pig poem in my poster," I said quickly.

There was no stopping us now. We worked separately. We worked together. We worked before school, during school, after school. After two weeks, our project was almost finished.

Becky had used LOTS of popsicle sticks for the pigsty.

Carlos had cut pop cans in half lengthways to make feeding troughs. Then he'd glued the two halves back-to-back so the top half formed a trough and the underneath formed a stand.

Tan's pigs were *so* cool. He'd painted them pale pink then drawn tiny flowers all over them — you could just faintly see the newsprint underneath. Each pig was different, but they all had smirky smiles on their faces, and cute curly tails made from recycled twist-ties.

Jodie's flying pig poem was the inspiration for my poster. First I painted the whole background blue. Then I painted a pig flying through clouds across the top — a pink, flowery pig to match Tan's models, except my pig had wings! Underneath the pig, in large letters, I painted part of our slogan:

DON'T HAM THINGS UP.

Beneath that I wrote Jodie's poem, in my best calligraphy. Below that, I painted the second part of the slogan:

KEEP THE SCENE CLEAN.

RECYCLE.

I mounted the poster on plywood so we could prop it behind the pigsty to form a backdrop.

Chapter 6

And the Winners Are...

The big day arrived. Mrs. Pinney led our class down the street to the Town Hall, where all of the projects were to be judged. There were three age-group categories — junior, intermediate, and senior.

We hardly spoke as we set our project up in our allocated space in the intermediate section.

I made sure my poster backdrop was firmly propped behind the pigsty.

Becky checked that none of her popsicle sticks had come unglued.

Carlos emptied a packet of unpopped popcorn into his pig troughs.

Tan looked his pigs over, then stood them in place around the troughs.

Finally, Jodie handed each of us one of her poem picket signs. We all chose a pig and stuck a sign through the coils of its curly tail. Then we all stood back and looked at our project.

Mrs. Pinney smiled at us. "I'm proud of you all," she said. "You've worked well individually, and you've been a great team."

I felt good. I could tell that the others did, too. "Even if we don't win," I thought, "it's been *lots* of fun!"

The judges deliberated for several days. The results were to be announced at a special presentation at the Town Hall. On that night, Jodie and I and our parents met the others early, so we could all sit together.

The first part of the evening came and went — I didn't pay much attention. My mind was flying ahead to the moment when they'd make the big announcement.

The junior prize winners were announced first. Five beaming kids filed onto the stage to claim their helicopter-ride vouchers.

The intermediate section was next. The microphone boomed, "And the winners are… "

We'd won!

We couldn't believe it. We sprang out of our seats. We jumped up and down. We waved our hands in the air. We danced down the aisle and pranced onto the stage.

One of the judges stepped up to the microphone. "These children designed and constructed a project so imaginative and humorous that the other judges and I decided we would like the children, their ideas, and their project to be part of a television campaign promoting recycling." He turned to us. "What was the inspiration for your project?"

Four of us looked at our "inspiration," and answered together — "JODIE!"

Once I lived on the most boring street in town...